Goldilocks and the Three Bears

A Publication of the World Language Division

Editor-in-Chief: Judith Bittinger

Project Director: Elinor Chamas

Editorial Development: Elly Schottman

Production/Manufacturing: James W. Gibbons

Cover and Text Design/Art Direction: Taurins Design Associates, New York

Illustrator: Karen Schmidt

ISBN 0-201-19055-9

14 15-WR-96 95

Addison-Wesley Publishing Company

Reading, Massachusetts • Menlo Park, California • New York • Don Mills, Ontario • Wokingham, England
Amsterdam • Bonn • Sydney • Singapore • Tokyo • Madrid • San Juan

Once upon a time,
there were three bears,
a  , a  , and a  .
One day the three bears
sat down to breakfast.

"This 🥣 is too hot!"
said 🐻 .

"This 🥣 is too hot!"
said 🐻 .

"This 🥣 is too hot!"
said 🐻 .

"Let's go for a walk,"
said 🐻 . "When we

come back, our 🥣
will be just right."

3

Along came 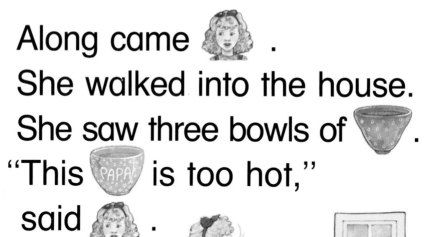 .
She walked into the house.
She saw three bowls of 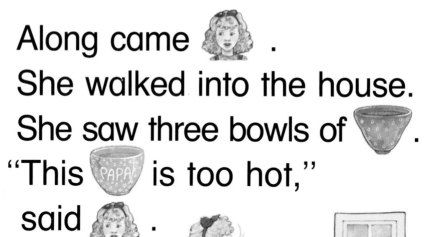 .
"This 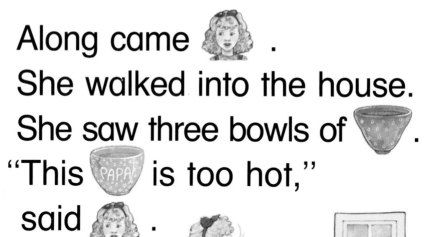 is too hot,"
said 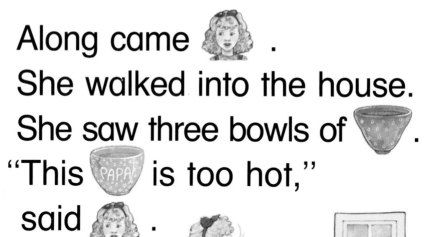 .

"This 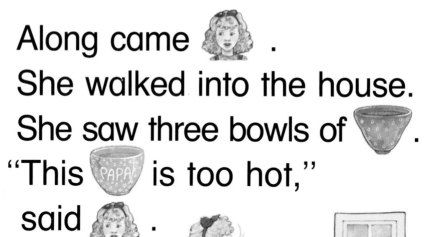 is too cold,"
said 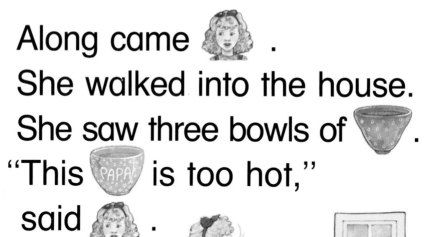 .

"This  is just right!'
said  .
And she ate it all up.

Then  went into
the living room.
She saw three chairs.
"This is too hard,"
said

"This is too soft,"
said

"This  is just right!"
said  .
Then CRASH
the  broke!

felt tired.

She went into the bedroom.

She saw three beds.

"This is too hard,"
said  .

"This  is too soft,"
said  .

"This  is just right,"
said  .
And she fell fast asleep.

The three bears came home.
They went into the kitchen.
"Someone's been eating
my  ," said  .

"Someone's been eating
my  ," said  .
"Someone's been eating
my  ," said  .
"And they ate it all up!"

The three bears went
into the living room.
"Someone's been sitting in
my  !" said  .

'Someone's been sitting in my !" said  .
'Someone's been sitting in my  ," said  .
'And now it's broken!"

The three bears went
into the bedroom.
"Someone's been sleeping in
my  !" said  .

"Someone's been sleeping in my !" said .
"Someone's been sleeping in my ," said .
"And here she is!"

 woke up.
She saw three angry bears
looking at her.
 jumped out of bed.
She ran out of the house.
And she never came
back again!